HELLO, I'M THEA!

I'm *Geronimo Stilton*'s sister. As I'm sure you know from my brother's bestselling novels, I'm a special correspondent for *The Rodent's Gazette*, Mouse Island's most famous newspaper. Unlike my 'fraidy mouse brother, I absolutely adore traveling, having adventures, and meeting rodents from all around the world!

The adventure I want to tell you about begins at Mouseford Academy, the school I went to when I was a young mouseling. I had such a great experience there as a student that I came back to teach a journalism class.

When I returned as a grown mouse, I met five really special students: Colette, Nicky, Pamela, Paulina, and Violet. You could hardly imagine five more different mouselings, but they became great friends right away. And they liked me so much that they decided to name their group after me: the Thea Sisters! I was so touched by that, I decided to write about their adventures. So turn the page to read a fabumouse adventure about the

THEA SISTERS!

Colette

She has a passion for clothing and style, especially anything pink. When she grows up, she wants to be a fashion editor.

Paulina

Cheerful and kind, she loves traveling and meeting rodents from all over the world. She has a magic touch when it comes to technology.

Violet

She's the bookworm of the group, and she loves learning. She enjoys classical music and dreams of becoming a famouse violinist.

Nicky

She comes from Australia and is very enthusiastic about sports and nature. She loves being outside and is always ready to get up and go!

Pamela

She is a great mechanic: Give her a screwdriver and she'll fix anything! She loves pizza, which she eats every day, and she loves to cook.

Do you want to help the Thea Sisters in this new adventure? It's not hard — just follow the clues!

When you see this magnifying glass, pay attention: It means there's an important clue on the page. Each time one appears, we'll review the clues so we don't miss anything.

**ARE YOU READY?
A NEW MYSTERY AWAITS!**

Geronimo Stilton

Thea Stilton
AND THE VENICE MASQUERADE

Scholastic Inc.

Copyright © 2016 by Edizioni Piemme S.p.A., Palazzo Mondadori, Via Mondadori 1, 20090 Segrate, Italy. International Rights © Atlantyca S.p.A. English translation © 2017 by Atlantyca S.p.A.

The publisher does not have any control over and does not assume any responsibility for author or third-party websites or their content.

GERONIMO STILTON and THEA STILTON names, characters, and related indicia are copyright, trademark, and exclusive license of Atlantyca S.p.A. All rights reserved. The moral right of the author has been asserted. Based on an original idea by Elisabetta Dami. www.geronimostilton.com

Published by Scholastic Inc., *Publishers since 1920*, 557 Broadway, New York, NY 10012. SCHOLASTIC and associated logos are trademarks and/or registered trademarks of Scholastic Inc.

Stilton is the name of a famous English cheese. It is a registered trademark of the Stilton Cheese Makers' Association. For more information, go to www.stiltoncheese.com.

ISBN 978-1-338-15923-3

Text by Thea Stilton
Original title *Carnevale a Venezia*
Cover by Caterina Giorgetti (design) and Flavio Ferron (color)
Illustrations by Barbara Pellizzari (design) and Flavio Ferron (color)
Graphics by Giovanna Ferraris and Paola Berardelli

Special thanks to Beth Dunfey
Translated by Emily Clement
Interior design by Kay Petronio

10 9 8 7 6 5 4 3 2 1   17 18 19 20 21

Printed in the U.S.A.   40
First printing 2017

A PLACE
OF DREAMS

There are certain cities in the world that are LEGENDARY. Every rodent has heard about these cities — and dreamed of visiting them.

We've all seen pictures of these places. We've heard stories about them. But there's nothing like being there in the fur for the first time.

That's how it was for the Thea Sisters — best friends Colette, Nicky, Pam, Paulina, and Violet — when their train pulled into the magical city of Venice, Italy!

The view before them was incredible. Outside the train station was a wide, open piazza overlooking a canal. The sparkling water was so close you could dive right in. And the elegant buildings on the other side of the canal seemed to float on the water.

"Holey cheese! This is even more spectacular than I imagined," Violet murmured.

Her friends agreed. Their

Wow!

It's gorgeous!

journey from Whale Island had been filled with **misadventures**. Their flight had been bumpy, and the turbulence got so bad they'd had to land in Milan. From there they'd boarded a **train** to Venice.

But the hassle was worth it: Venice, that enchanting city on the water, lay gleaming before them in all its majesty.

What a marvemouse city!

"Thank goodmouse we've finally arrived," Nicky said. "Where do we go from here?"

Paulina fished out her MousePad. She'd downloaded a GUIDEBOOK before they left Mouseford Academy, the school all five mouselets attended.

"Let me check Elisa and Marco's address . . ."

The previous year, the Thea Sisters had made two new friends during Mouseford's SUMMER session.

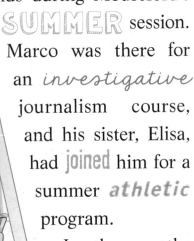

See you in Venice!

Marco was there for an *investigative* journalism course, and his sister, Elisa, had joined him for a summer *athletic* program.

In the months

afterward, they'd kept In touch with the Thea Sisters, and a few weeks earlier Marco and Elisa had invited the mouselets to visit Venice, their hometown, to take part in the famouse Carnival!

When the Thea Sisters received their invitation, the mouselets were so excited, they started jumping up and down like baby bunnies. Colette couldn't wait to see Carnival's famous M·A·S·K·S and fancy costumes. Pam's belly started rumbling at the thought of all those delicious fritterS. Paulina and Violet were dying to EXPLORE the canals, and Nicky wanted to learn how to steer a gondola.

"Here we go," said Paulina, reading from her book. "Let's head for Calle del Paradiso. Elisa and Marco's house should be close."

"Calle del Paradiso . . . the streets of Venice have such **marvemouse** names."

Colette sighed, admiring the sparkling sunshine on the water. "It's all so romantic . . ."

"Sure, it's *romantic*, but how in the name of string cheese are we going to get there?" Pam asked. "There aren't any buses here, and no taxis, either."

"Oh, there are taxis here." Paulina smiled. "They're just not cars . . . they're boats!" She pointed to a wooden boat with a yellow flag on its prow.

"Well, what are we waiting for?" Nicky

asked. "Let's shake a tail!

VENICE
is calling!"

A TAXI WITHOUT WHEELS

The Thea Sisters scurried on board the wateʀ taxi and gave the driver their friends' address. Then Paulina pulled out her *MousePad* again.

"So, this must be the Grand Canal, the ancient canal that divides the city into two parts. Over there is a church . . . and now we're passing under a bridge. It must be . . . the Bridge . . ."

This is the Grand Canal!

"The Bridge of the Barefoot!" explained a friendly ratlet seated next to the taxi driver. "You mouselets have

8

just **arrived** in town, right?"

Nicky nodded. "Yes, this is our first time in Venice."

"Then you're LUCKY you're on this boat," the ratlet replied. "Venice is best seen from the water. You get a great view of the architecture."

"When was the city built?" asked Violet.

Paulina checked her MousePad again. "Well, according to my guide, most buildings date from the thirteen hundreds . . . but also the fourteen hundreds . . ."

". . . and all the centuries after that," the ratlet cut in again. "Here in Venice, you can see architecture from every era. On our left, for example, is Ca' Pesaro, **built** between the seventheeth and eighteenth centuries for the Pesaro family. That's how it got its name."

"My guidebook says the Museum of Modern Art is inside Ca' Pesaro," Paulina added.

"That's right! There are more than TEN public museums in the city," the ratlet said.

"I have a complete list," said Paulina.

Her friends gathered around her to take a look. Violet, who adored art, let out an enthusiastic squeak. "The seventeenth century in Venice . . . there are so many mousterpieces I can't wait to see!"

"I'd like to visit the Museum of Natural History," Nicky added.

"What about the Lace Museum?! We can't miss that," Colette put in.

"Um . . . mouselets . . ." the ratlet said.

"Hey, Pam, which museum do you want to visit?" Paulina asked her friend.

"Mouselets . . ." the ratlet repeated.

"Isn't there one that's all about ships and seafaring?" asked Pam. "I'd like to check that out."

"**MOUSELETS!**" the ratlet squeaked at the top of his lungs.

The Thea Sisters finally lifted their snouts from the MousePad screen. The ratlet had his paws spread out in front of him, **displaying** a spectacular view of the city before them.

"Pardon the **interruption**, but don't you want to see the *real* city of **Venice** instead of just looking at a bunch of pictures on your MousePad?" he asked.

Paulina turned redder than a cheese rind. She quickly tucked away her **MOUSEPAD**. "You're right!"

"Hey, what's that?" asked Pam.

Just ahead of them, a majestic stone bridge with an elegant colonnade spanned the canal.

"That's the oldest bridge in Venice," the ratlet explained. "The Rialto."

"You've almost reached your destination," said the taxi driver, steering the motorboat to one side so the mouselets could enjoy the view. "The address you're looking for is just up AHEAD."

This is the Rialto!

Venice

Venice is an archipelago of over one hundred islands that occupies a LAGOON on the northern end of the Adriatic Sea. It is connected to the Italian mainland by a long bridge.

Since Venice is MADE MOSTLY OF ISLANDS, residents navigate the city using a SYSTEM OF CANALS (more than one hundred fifty in all!). There are over FOUR HUNDRED BRIDGES spanning the many canals.

Venice's largest canal is the majestic GRAND CANAL, which is over TWO MILES long. It crosses the entire city in an enormous backward S shape.

The waters of Venice's lagoon often rise so high that they flood the city's streets and piazzas. This is known as ACQUA ALTA (high water). When *acqua alta* occurs, wooden walkways are placed over the squares and streets so residents and tourists can make their way across.

A HOUSE ON THE WATER

After the motorboat passed the Rialto, the driver stopped in front of a pink building. "Here we are! This is the house you're looking for."

The lower part of the building was covered in **scratched-up** bricks. A small dock led from the edge of the canal to the front door.

"Jumping tuna fish, check it out. Our friends live right on the water!" Pam exclaimed.

"How do they get around? By taxi?" asked Colette.

"With that," replied Paulina, nodding at a small wooden boat tied up next to the door.

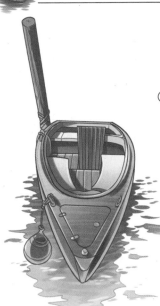

"Thea Sisters, you're here!" cried a cheerful squeak.

The mouselets looked up. Leaning over a small balcony above their snouts was their friend Marco, waving happily. Behind him was his sister, Elisa.

"We'll come down and let you in," Marco called.

"Maybe life in Venice isn't so different from other cities," Pam reflected. "It just has canals instead of streets and boats instead of cars!"

"That's right, Pam," Marco replied, throwing open the front door. "The only problem is the acqua alta. I hope you brought rubber boots."

"Marco!" cried Pam, leaping to hug her friend.

Soon the **SIBLINGS'** house was filled with happy chatter. The rodents had a lot to catch up on. Marco and Elisa peppered the Thea Sisters with questions, and the mouselets told them all the latest news from Mouseford Academy and their first impressions of Venice.

Marco and Elisa led their friends into the dining room. "We figured you'd be **starving** after your long trip," Elisa said.

As if on cue, Pam's stomach let out a noisy rumble.

"So we made you a SNACK!" Marco said, emerging from the kitchen with a big tray of cheesy chow.

A few moments later, the Thea Sisters were

nibbling on the local dishes their friends had prepared.

"We're so **LUCKY** you love to cook," Pam commented, serving herself some rice with **peas**. "What did you say this dish was called?"

Glad you like it!

This food is great!

"Risi e bisi," Marco replied.

"It's good, but I prefer this yummy spaghetti with beans," Colette said.

"It's called bigoli," Elisa explained. "It's a traditional Venetian pasta shape."

"And this *baccalà* is tastier than toasted Brie!" added Nicky as she reached for a second portion.

"Glad you like it," Marco said. "Now, eat up — you're going to need lots of energy because we're going to walk your paws off. We've got dozens of parades, parties, and masquerades lined up."

"Marco, don't scare them . . ." Elisa said.

"They're not scared! They're here for the world-famous Carnival of Venice, after all," Marco replied.

"That's right," Nicky cheered. "And we're ready to party!"

Violet nodded. "We can't wait!"

"Squeaking of which . . ." Marco said, looking at his watch, "we better get going."

"Let's go!" cried Nicky, springing to her paws faster than a gerbil on a wheel. "Are we taking your boat?"

"Yes, but don't you want to change?" Marco replied.

The mouselets LOOKED down at their clothes. Their outfits were rumpled from the long trip

"I guess we should freshen up. My fur is a total MESS, right?" Colette said, blushing pinker than cat's nose.

Is my fur messed up?!

Marco laughed and shook his snout. "No, it's not that. I meant you might want to put on some costumes for Carnival."

LIKE A DREAM!

Elisa led the mouselets to a closet bursting with spangled, sequined costumes. "Let's look in here," she said, pulling out a large box.

Colette's eyes grew rounder than twin wheels of cheese when she spotted all the silky fabrics, colorful feathers, and gold-embroidered shoes. You see, Colette had a true passion for fashion.

"Wow! It's like a treasure chest!"

Elisa took out a blue-and-silver dress with a crescent-shaped mask.

The moon . . .

"This is my costume this year:
THE MOON!"

"I'll be my sister's opposite,"
Marco said, pulling out
a *fabumouse* yellow-and-
orange suit and a mask
with golden rays.

. . . and the sun!

"The sun," cried
Colette, clapping her
paws. "I love it!"

"These are all the costumes
our family has used over the last
few years," Elisa explained,
indicating the box of **colorful**
garments. "Pick any costume you
like. We'll see you in a half hour.

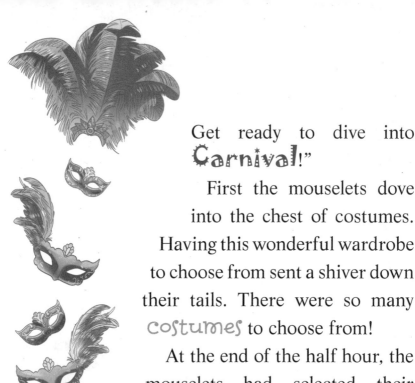

Get ready to dive into Carnival!"

First the mouselets dove into the chest of costumes. Having this wonderful wardrobe to choose from sent a shiver down their tails. There were so many costumes to choose from!

At the end of the half hour, the mouselets had selected their **outfits**. Colette wore a *springtime* gown embroidered with dozens of tiny flowers; Paulina wore a turquoise costume with coral designs and a **fish** mask; Pam choose a big orange cloak with a **lion's** mane; Nicky wore a dress and mask that made her look

like a *butterfly*; and Violet had selected a costume covered with tiny **musical** notes.

When Marco and Elisa returned, they gave their friends the paws-up sign. "You're definitely ready for **Carnival**. Let's go!" said Elisa.

Colette, Nicky, Pam, Paulina, and Violet had heard a lot about Carnival. But what they discovered went far beyond anything they'd dared to imagine. The Thea Sisters and their friends were immediately drawn into a *noisy*, JOYOUS throng of rodents, all of whom were dressed in splendid **masks** and multicolored, sparkling COSTUMES. There was singing and laughter everywhere they looked.

Pam was so busy rodent-watching, she accidentally bumped into a passerby wearing a bizarre mask with a LoNg NoSe. "Oops, excuse me!" she apologized.

The masked mouse turned and, without squeaking a word, bowed deeply.

Then he disappeared into the crowd.

"Hey . . . where'd he go?" Pam wondered. It was almost as if she'd DREAMED the encounter.

Elisa smiled. "The city is full of magic during Carnival. You'll often wonder if what you're seeing is real."

Meanwhile, the mice had reached a LARGE square surrounded by warmly lit buildings.

"This is Piazza San Marco, the most famous square in the city," said Elisa.

"And we're here just in time for the Gran Teatro parade!" added her brother.

The Thea Sisters marveled at the masks of the rodents around them. Paulina snapped photos of everyone who scurried by.

Then, suddenly, they heard a shout. "Ahhhhhhhhhhh! Hellllllp!"

The cry of distress was coming from a female rodent in an elaborate eighteenth century costume.

"What happened?" asked Colette, rushing to her side. A small, curious crowd formed around her.

"They've **ROBBED** me! They've taken my precious . . . my precious . . ."

". . . pocketbook?" Pam guessed.

"Noooo!" the rodent wailed.

"My precious **FAN!**"

THE MISSING FAN

The mouselets **LOOKED** surprised. The rodent continued moaning in misery.

"Who took it?" asked Nicky.

"How should I know?!" the female rodent replied. "I just know my **fan** is gone!"

"We'll help you. Can you tell us what happened?" Paulina asked.

The rodent **sighed** and began her tale. "I was watching the parade when something **shiny** on the ground caught my eye. It looked like a jeweled pin. I figured it must have **fallen** off a costume, so I leaned over to **PiCK** it up." She pointed to the skirt of her **magnificent** gown. "I stowed my **fan** in this pocket. When I stood up again . . . it was gone!"

"And you didn't notice anyone around?" Violet asked.

The rodent shook her snout. "No way! I would never let someone **steal** my fan. It was **a master thief**, I tell you! In place of my fan, I found this CARD in my pocket." She showed them a card with a top hat in the CENTER.

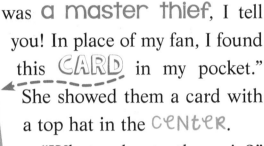

"What about the pin?" asked Violet.

The rodent shook her snout. "That's the strangest part of all. It disappeared, too. Before I could pick it up, it vanished!"

"Maybe someone kicked it away?" Marco suggested. "With the **crowd** today that's definitely possible . . . And the same thing probably happened to your **fan** . . ."

The rodent gave him a SCORNFUL

look. "Young ratlet, if my fan had simply **SLIPPED** out of my pocket, I would have realized it. But it **disappeared**! I assure you I am telling the truth!"

"**Moldy mozzarella**," Pam muttered, scratching her snout. "What kind of **MAGIC** is this?"

Marco checked the ground all **AROUND** the rodent, but there was no trace of the fan.

"Was it *valuable*?" asked Paulina.

"Not particularly, although it was an antique. But it had great sentimental value. I carry it at

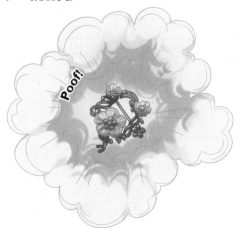

every **Carnival** . . . It's irreplaceable!"
the rodent lamented.

"And you didn't notice anything else
unusual?" Violet asked.

The rodent **shook** her snout. Then she
stopped and stared as if she'd just had a
revelation.

"Actually . . ." she began, "there was one
thing, but I don't know if . . ."

"Tell us," Nicky urged her. "Even the
smallest **detail** could be useful."

"When I leaned over to pick up the pin, I heard a sound like **flapping wings**," the rodent said.

"Well, there are a lot of pigeons around here," Pam commented.

"I've never heard a pigeon that noisy," the rodent said. "I want to go home now."

She hurried away, leaving the mouselets and their friends confused and intrigued.

"I don't know what you rats think, but something here doesn't add up," Colette said.

Paulina nodded. "The mysterious card, the sound of **flapping wings** . . ."

I heard flapping wings . . .

"Why would anyone STEAL a fan?" Violet asked. "The square is filled with hundreds of rodents wearing necklaces and tiaras that are much more **valuable**."

No one had **AN ANSWER**. Finally, Marco squeaked up. "Maybe the fan fell into the CANAL. Come on, we can't let this spoil our evening. We should watch the parade and then head home for dinner."

"Let's scurry along, then," said Pam, laughing. "I'm already as peckish as a porcupine!"

Him Again!

As the seven friends opened the door to Elisa and Marco's house, a deep squeak **greeted** them. "Elisa, Marco, are you back? And did your **friends** arrive?"

The lean snout of a tall, **bearded** rodent poked out of the door to the kitchen.

"Papa!" cried Elisa, throwing her paws around him. "You're home **early**!"

The corners of her father's serious snout lifted in an affectionate

Is that you?

smile. "I was able to leave the police station a bit early, so I made **dinner** for you. Aren't you going to introduce me to your friends?"

"Oh, of course!" Elisa said. "This is Colette, Violet, Nicky, Pam, and Paulina, otherwise known as . . ."

". . . the Thea Sisters!" the mouselets finished, stepping forward to introduce themselves.

The mouselets and their friends quickly changed out of their costumes. Then they gathered around the table for dinner.

"So you are a policemouse?" Colette asked their friends' father.

Elisa answered for him. "Oh, no, he's the chief inspector. And he's so busy solving cases that we hardly ever **SEE** him."

Her father laughed. "Elisa is exaggerating,

but it's true that my work has kept me very busy lately. There's been a lot of crime in Venice."

"We witnessed a minor theft today," Violet told him.

"What kind of theft?" the inspector asked.

"Oh, nothing **VALUABLE** . . ." replied Pam. "Just an antique **fan** belonging to an eighteenth century rodent. That is," she corrected herself, "the rodent wasn't from the eighteenth century, but her *dress* was."

"Tell me more," said the inspector. "And please, don't leave out any details."

When Pam described the card with the top hat, the inspector threw his napkin on the table in frustration. "**HiM AGAiN!**" he exclaimed.

"Him . . . who?" Elisa asked.

"Oh, it's NOTHING. Nothing you young

rodents need to worry your snouts about," her father replied.

Colette looked at her friends. Then she squeaked the words that were on all the Thea Sisters' minds. "Sir, we have a lot of experience solving Mysteries. We might be able to help you . . . and I promise we won't tell anyone about your investigation."

The inspector gazed at the mouselets and his children for a moment. Then he SIGHED. "Very well. For the last few days, MASKS and other antique costume accessories have gone missing from all over the city, and we don't have any leads. Locating the thief has been harder than finding a cheese slice in a haystack! All the thefts have taken place under MYSTERIOUS circumstances . . . in the blink of a cat's eye, without anyone noticing anything, the objects just disappear."

"Like today, with the fan and the pin the rodent saw on the ground," Violet reflected.

The inspector nodded. "Each time, the only trace left by this RAT BURGLAR is a card like the one you described."

"Like a signature!" Pamela cried. "But what does it mean?"

The inspector shook his snout. "We don't know."

"What else has he STOLEN?" Marco said.

The inspector pulled a yellow file folder out of his bag and showed them a stack of photographs. "These are some of the stolen objects," he said.

Everyone gathered around to get a better LOOK. There was a splendid peacock MASK, a mask covered in seashells, and a luxurious golden costume.

"Hmm . . . do these things have anything in common?" Colette wondered.

"NO, it doesn't look like it," Marco replied. "But there must be something! First we should find out who they belong to . . ."

The inspector quickly put the photos back into the folder.

"No, no, I can't get you mouselings involved in this," he declared. "I've already TOLD you too much."

"But, Papa . . ." Marco said. "We just want to help you."

"You know you can't help with my work. It's too dangerous." Then, **softening** a bit, he added, "I am going back to the station to **gather** information on the case. See you later, okay?"

With that, he *SCURRIED AWAY*.

CLUES!

THE MYSTERIOUS THIEF'S SIGNATURE IS A TOP HAT . . . COULD THAT BE A CLUE?

THE ITEMS IN THE INSPECTOR'S PHOTOGRAPHS ALL HAD SOMETHING IN COMMON. DID YOU NOTICE WHAT IT WAS?

THE GRAND PARADE

The tense moment was soon forgotten. After dinner, Elisa and Marco *told* their friends about the **BIG EVENING** they'd planned.

"First, we were thinking about a *beauty contest*," said Marco.

"A beauty contest? Does Carnival always include events *like that*?" asked Colette.

Marco laughed. "Yes, but, don't worry, there's a twist. It's a competition to see who has the most beautiful **mask**!"

"The competition takes place every year," his sister explained. "Tonight we'll get to see all the contestants. You're going to love it — it's one of my favorite parts of Carnival. Come on, let's get back in costume!"

When the mouselets and their friends **returned** to Piazza San Marco, it was **more luminous** than ever in the soft evening light.

On the stage of the Gran Teatro, a line of

rodents **dressed** as ladies, knights, ancient Egyptians, wild animals, and dozens of other fantastic creatures paraded by to the beat of DRUMS.

The Thea Sisters stopped to ADMIRE the incredible costumes strolling by on the catwalk.

The mouselets gasped

Amazing!

in admiration along with the happy and colorful crowd around them.

"This is better than a fashion show, right, Coco?" Pam joked.

Colette laughed. "Well, this parade has the most outrageous fashions I've ever seen."

"You're right. This NIGHT is so magical, I wish it would never end," Nicky added.

Marco and Elisa smiled and exchanged a look.

"Well, it's not over yet. We have another idea," Marco began.

A party!

"If you're interested in one more surprise," Elisa said, nodding.

"But maybe you're too tired," her brother teased the mouselets.

"Tired? Us? You must be pulling our paws," said Pam.

"Come on, don't keep us in suspense," Paulina said eagerly. "What's next?"

"A party!" Marco cried.

"A party? Of course we're not too tired! We're fresher than new mozzarella and as ENERGETIC as baby bunnies!" Colette cheered, clapping her paws.

"Some of papa's FRIENDS are holding a masked ball," Elisa began.

Pam didn't let her finish. "Well, what are we waiting for?

A PARTY . . .
WITH A SURPRISE

A half hour later, the Thea Sisters, Marco, and Elisa **scampered** into a luxurious building that was all done up for Carnival.

When the friends reached the ballroom, they were struck **squeakless**: There were at least a hundred guests chattering and twirling across the floor, making their marvemouse costumes **shimmer**.

"Look **over there**, Marco, it's Papa," said Elisa. "Does he still look stressed?"

"No, don't worry. He'll be happy to see us," Marco reassured her.

The Thea Sisters strained to **SEE** the **POLICE** inspector. He was dressed in an elegant and elaborate, **old-fashioned** noblemouse's costume.

"Who is the **LADY RODENT** he's squeaking to?" asked Colette.

Next to the inspector was a rodent in an **antique** velvet dress, complete with an intricate headpiece that looked like it was made of ice.

"She's an old **FRIEND** of Papa's. She owns this place," explained Elisa. "Don't you love her dress? It represents **winter**."

What a great party!

"Her headpiece is the **rat's whiskers**," Colette gushed.

"We should take some pictures for our classes at the **Fashion Institute**," Paulina suggested. "The students would love these dresses!"

Before they could take out their MousePhones, the CRYSTAL chandeliers illuminating the ballroom suddenly went out, leaving the guests in DARKNESS. The music stopped, and a hush fell over the room.

"Mouselets! What's going on?" Elisa murmured, worried, feeling around for her friends' paws.

"Slimy Swiss balls! Coco? Nick? Where . . ." Pam began.

Just then, a female rodent's shout echoed through the room. "Aaaaaah!"

The lights suddenly came back on. In the center of the room, the lady of the house had her paws on the top of her snout. Her precious headpiece had DISAPPEARED!

The Thea Sisters rushed toward her. All around them, the room filled with whispers.

"It just . . . disappeared!"

"Like magic!"

"But how? Who could have taken it?"

Nicky pointed to the chandelier above the lady's snout. It was swaying back and forth, making the crystal drops clink together. There was a window open!

Just then, something fluttered through the air. Nicky reached out and grabbed it.

It was another card like the one they'd seen before — with the drawing of a **TOP HAT** in the center!

NEW CLUES

Nicky **TURNED** the card over in her paws.

"The mysterious thief again . . ." Paulina commented, COMING over to take a better look.

Violet turned to the lady of the house, who had **collapsed** into a pawchair. A look of despair crossed her snout. "Excuse me, but could you tell us what happened? Maybe we can help you," Violet said.

The rodent sighed. "I . . . honestly, I didn't notice anything. The lights went out . . . I heard a strange sound . . ."

"Like **flapping wings**?" Marco guessed, remembering the words of the rodent whose fan had been stolen.

"Actually, yes . . . how did you know that?"

the lady rodent asked in surprise.

Just then, the inspector appeared at her side. "What are you **doing**?" he asked his son.

"Just asking a few questions about how the headpiece was *stolen*," Marco replied.

What are you doing?

His father shook his snout. "I already told you not to worry about all this. It could be **DANGEROUS**!"

"But, Papa . . ." Elisa objected.

"Please, no arguments! Now you young rodents scurry along home. I'll ask the questions here," her father said sternly.

So the mouselets and their friends **LEFT** the party. But by the time they returned home, their snouts were spinning with questions. Instead of going to sleep, they gathered in the living room to talk about the case.

"We only have a few **CLUES**," Paulina began uncertainly.

"It's true," Marco said. "Like the card with the **TOP HAT**. . ."

"What could it mean?" asked Pam.

"It must be a kind of *signature*," Colette

guessed. "But that doesn't tell us much."

"Then there's the sound of **flapping wings**," Elisa added.

"And the ◯ⓟⓔⓝ window . . ." Violet said.

Pam yawned. "I don't know about you mice, but I'm sleepier than a sloth. Can we continue this conversation tomorrow morning over a nice big breakfast?"

Marco smiled. "If Pam is ready for a ratnap, then it's definitely time for bed." He scrambled to his paws, accidentally knocking over a table full of **notes**, books, and his father's folders. The yellow folder that the inspector had shown them earlier fell to the floor, spilling its contents onto the carpet.

"**Marco!**

Sometimes I

think you were born with two left paws," Elisa scolded him.

Violet began to **gather** up the documents. As she picked up a photo, she asked, "Hey, what does 𝕄𝕌ℝ𝔸ℕ𝕆 mean? It's written here beneath the photo of the stolen peacock mask."

Murano

"It's a place — an island not *far* from the city," Elisa explained.

"Isn't it famouse for its **GLASSWORK**?" Colette asked. "I think I read that in Paulina's guidebook."

"Yes, that's right," Elisa replied. "It's very famouse. In fact, it's one of the places we're planning to bring you to **visit**."

"Mouselets, I have an idea," Marco said. "Let's continue our *investigation* tomorrow on Murano."

Pam shook the sleep out of her eyes. "What do you have in mind?" she asked curiously.

Marco smiled. "You'll see!"

CLUES!

EVERYONE WHO'S HAD SOMETHING STOLEN HAS HEARD THE FLAPPING OF WINGS JUST BEFORE THE THEFT...

WHAT COULD THAT MEAN?

A Hidden Signature

The next morning, the Thea Sisters woke up early. They were very eager to see more of Venice — and to continue their investigation.

Marco's plan was simple: They would visit Murano and have a look around. He was hoping they'd find the owner of the peacock MASK and get to ask some questions.

But Elisa wasn't crazy about her brother's plan. As their vaporetto* zipped across the lagoon, she raised her objections. "Marco, let's just take the mouselets sightseeing. Our friends are here to have fun, not play DETECTIVE."

"But they're the greatest mystery experts we know," argued Marco, smiling warmly at the Thea Sisters. "Right, mouselets?"

*A vaporetto is a motorboat. It's the most common means of public transportation in Venice. It's used instead of buses.

"We do LOVE a good mystery," Violet agreed. "But Elisa is right. We want to see the city. Plus, we don't want to get you in TROUBLE with your father."

"Okay, okay," Marco gave in with a grin. "First some sight-seeing, and *then* some INVESTIGATING."

Pam laughed. "You're more stubborn than a shrew mouse!"

As the vaporetto drew closer to shore, Elisa began telling her friends a little about Murano. "Murano isn't just one island. It's **several** small islands connected by **BRIDGES** and canals," she explained. "It's world famouse for its glasswork. Our first stop is a factory devoted to this *tradition*."

Let's stick to sightseeing.

The mouselets and their friends scrambled off the vaporetto and headed straight for the glass FURNACE. "This is where the most respected glass masters in Venice work," Marco said.

Inside the factory, the friends watched a rodent working on a mass of white-hot glass. As he expertly turned the glass hunk, it was transformed into a magnificent vase.

"That's amazing!" cried Pam at last.

"You haven't seen anything yet," Marco said.

They entered an ancient palazzo. "This museum has some of the most important collections of glass from different eras," Elisa said.

"This place makes me more nervous than a rat in a cat clinic. I don't want to knock anything over," said Pam.

"Each piece is unique. Breaking something would be a **CAT-ASTROPHE**," Marco admitted.

Just then, they were interrupted by a shout from Colette. "Aaaaah!"

"Coco, are you okay?" Pam asked, scurrying over to her.

"Oh, no, I'm fine. Just look at this pink glass flamingo," her friend squealed. "It's simply divine!"

Pam grinned. "That's our Coco. She loves every color as long as it's pink," she told Elisa.

The two mouselets headed toward a case displaying a **MASK** made of glass. It was quite simple, with a delicate pink flower on one side, but the mouselets were struck by its elegance.

"It's so lovely," Pam said.

Her friends joined her to admire the mask. "Hey, look at that symbol just below the flower," Violet said.

"Which one?" asked Paulina. "That little sun?"

"Yes, I have a feeling I've seen it before, but I can't remember where . . ." Violet's squeak trailed off.

"On the stolen masks!" Paulina cried.

"Which masks?" Elisa asked, confused.

"The stolen masks and costumes that Papa showed us in those photos," Marco replied. "Now that you mention it, I noticed this symbol, too . . ."

"Maybe it's the mark of the artist," Violet guessed. She looked at the label next to the mask. "Look, there's a name here: Berto Del Bon."

Paulina typed the name into her MousePad.

"I found him! Berto Del Bon lived in the first half of the eighteenth century. He was an artist who **specialized** in costumes and masks. He worked for the most **important** families in Venice. He was highly respected, but then he had a disagreement with a rich merchant and ended up falling into DISGRACE. Then his work was largely forgotten . . ."

"But why?" Colette asked, CURIOUS.

Paulina continued reading. "Hmm, let me see. This merchant refused to sell goods to the poorest mice in the city. Then he asked Berto to create an elaborate peacock mask for him, but Berto made him a **turkey** mask instead!

"When he saw the mask, the merchant was more furious than a fly stuck in fondue. He swore revenge against Berto and vowed to erase his fame forever."

"**That's awful!**" Colette cried indignantly.

"True," Marco agreed. "But at least now we finally have a **CLUE**."

Violet nodded. "We know that the **mysterious thief** only steals works by Berto Del Bon."

TEA AND CLUES

After realizing what all the STOLEN objects had in common, the Thea Sisters couldn't get the mystery out of their minds.

The little group headed to the home of the peacock mask's owner. Marco had discovered the address in their father's FILES. The apartment was on Murano, on the top floor of a six story-building with no elevator.

"This . . . puff . . . Venetian investigation . . . pant . . . sure is exhausting . . ." Colette gasped.

Nicky, *ATHLETIC* as always, cheered on the others from above. She'd scrambled up the stairs faster than the mouse who ran up the clock.

When they finally Reached the top floor,

Marco knocked on the door. A moment later, it was opened . . . by a swan!

Colette, Nicky, Pam, Paulina, Violet, Elisa, and Marco were **SURPRISED** for a moment. Then they realized it was just a **costume**. Behind the swan's mask was a short rodent with white fur that **blended in** with his feathered headpiece.

"Um . . . hello . . ." Marco said. "We're investigating the **theft** of a peacock mask, and I believe

Come on, guys!

it belonged to you . . ."

"That's right," the rodent said sadly.

"Could we ask you some **questions**?" Pam asked.

The rodent nodded. "Of course. I was just making some tea."

One wall of the rodent's mousehole was completely **covered** by a precious costume collection. Colette gazed up at it. "Why . . . these are all bird costumes."

The older rodent smiled. "That's right. I've collected bird masks for years. This swan mask is new."

"Um, it really suits you . . ." Colette said.

"Oh, I'm such a

sillysnout! I forgot I still had it on, **HA, HA!** I was just trying it on for the first time when you rang the bell," the rodent replied.

"Gotcha," Pam said. "For a minute, I thought you always **dressed** like that."

Nicky stepped on her paw, whispering, "*Shh!*" She pointed to a costume that was missing its mask. "Does this outfit go with the peacock mask?"

The rodent nodded. "I found that mask by **CHANCE** at a market recently," he explained. "It dates back to the eighteenth century. The artist is not well known, but he was very *skilled* . . ."

"**Berto Del Bon**," said Paulina.

"Exactly! The moment I saw it, I knew I had to wear it to Carnival. So I brought it home and tried it on. But then . . ."

"But then?" **prodded** Pam.

"Someone knocked on the door. That **SURPRISED** me, because I don't often have visitors. And when I opened the door . . ."

"No one was there?" Violet guessed.

The older rodent nodded. "But there was something on the doormat.

A small, shiny object. I leaned down to pick it up . . ."

"And it flew away," Nicky continued.

"Along with your MASK," Paulina finished.

"Exactly! How did you know?" the rodent asked in astonishment.

What beautiful costumes!

"Other THEFTS have followed the same pattern," Colette explained. "Did you find a strange card on the doormat?"

The rodent took a TOP HAT card out of a box. "Here it is. And there's something else."

"You heard wings flapping?" Elisa guessed.

"No, I don't have very good hearing. But my sight is still good . . ."

"You mean you saw the thief?!" Marco cried.

The rodent shook his snout. "No, but I saw this feather twirling above the staircase." He showed them a LARGE, shiny black feather.

"Did you notice anything else?" Marco asked.

"No, sorry," the rodent said.

"Don't **worry**. You've been very helpful," Violet thanked him. She and her friends said their good-byes.

"I hope you solve this MYSTERY . . . and find my mask!" the rodent said.

STATUS REPORT

• THE THIEF ONLY STEALS PIECES BY BERTO DEL BON.

• THEY DISTRACT THEIR VICTIMS BY SHOWING THEM AN OBJECT THAT QUICKLY APPEARS AND THEN DISAPPEARS.

• SO FAR THE CLUES ARE: FLAPPING WINGS, A LARGE BLACK FEATHER, AND THE TOP HAT CARD.

SECRET IDENTITY

The mouselets and their friends scurried to catch a vaporetto back to Venice. On the way, they reviewed the thief's *profile*:

They only steal works by **Berto Del Bon**.

Each time they steal something . . .

They leave a card with a **TOP HAT**.

And a **BLACK FEATHER**!

Violet had been quiet as a mouse as her friends had chattered away. Then, suddenly, she declared, "I know who the thief is."

"What?!" Nicky cried in disbelief.

"I take that back," Violet said. "I don't know who it is, but I have a good guess. Think about it: Who usually wears a **TOP HAT**?"

Her friends stared at her in confusion.

"Here's another clue," Violet said. "The disappearances almost seem like magic. And who usually performs tricks using sleight of paw?"

"Of course! It must be a magician," Pam shouted.

"What about the **BLACK FEATHER**?" asked Colette.

"Our magician must have a black bird of some kind . . . maybe a raven," Violet suggested.

"Um, I don't want to **throw mold** over your cheese," Elisa interrupted, "but does it help us to know that the **thief** is dressed like a **magician**?"

"Uh-huh! Because now we know we need to track down magicians," Marco cried, beaming.

"We need to tell your dad," Violet said. "This **clue** could help his investigation."

Elisa sighed. "Maybe. But he's going to be

Papa will get mad!

grouchier than a groundhog when he hears what we've been up to. We're in for a serious **lecture**!"

Elisa was right. That evening, the inspector listened attentively to the young rodents' revelations. But when they were finished telling their tale, his squeak took a **severe** tone. "Now, didn't I tell you not to get involved in this **investigation**?"

"But, Papa . . . we just want to help you. And look how many clues we've found!" Marco protested.

"Clues, notes, **vague ideas**," his father replied. "But you went against my wishes and knocked on a stranger's door. What if this magician turns out to be dangerous?"

"But we . . . **we wanted** . . ." Elisa stuttered.

"It's our fault, Inspector," said Pam. "We got too involved, and we disobeyed you."

Elisa and Marco's father sighed. "Okay, there's no point in discussing it. Just promise me you'll leave this alone. For the next few days, just enjoy Carnival. Otherwise, I'll be forced to ground you."

No more investigations!

"What?!" Marco burst out.

His father strode through the door, declaring, "I have to head back to the station. But don't forget what I told you."

Elisa sighed. "Oh dear. Now Papa is madder than a cat with a bad case of fleas!

Marco, we should have listened to him . . ."

The mouselets were **sorry** they'd helped get their friends in trouble. Colette, Nicky, Paulina, and Violet tried to cheer up Elisa. But Pam followed Marco, who'd scurried away in **ANGER**.

She found him in his room. "Can I come in?" she asked from the entrance.

Marco nodded. He looked glummer than a gerbil without a wheel. "My father is impossible," he complained. "He's so Stubborn! Whenever he has an idea, he acts like everyone should just go along with it."

"Reminds me of someone I know . . ." said Pam.

"Who?" Marco asked.

"Let's see. Well, someone who really believes in his ideas. Someone who's willing to go to the other side of Venice just to follow a lead . . ." she replied with a grin.

Marco *smiled*. "You're right. I'm just like my father. So why won't he take me seriously?"

"He will. He just thinks you're too young to be a detective," Pam said.

"But one day I'll surprise him," said Marco. "I just want him to be proud of me."

"I'm sure he already is," Pam reassured him.

"If you say so . . ." Marco sighed.

"We should talk more about this later, OKAY?" said Pam. "But for now, let's get back to our

"

THE MAGIC SHOP

The next day, the Thea Sisters and their friends explored Venice from one end to the other. They went to the Doge's Palace and the Ca' Rezzonico museum, where Violet admired the

Canaletto,
Rio dei Mendicanti

magnificent collection of paintings and ancient sculptures.

Then it was time for some SHOPPING. Colette wanted to bring back presents for all their friends. She went on a spree, buying glass knickknacks shaped like animals, tiny Venetian masks, and tons of postcards.

"Coco, when you shop, YOU DON'T STOP," Nicky said with a laugh.

Colette grinned. "I'm kind of a shopping specialist. Now I just need one last gift for my friend in Paris . . ."

"Check out that store," Pam said, pointing to a small window decorated with MULTICOLORED butterflies.

A mannequin dressed in a gorgeous dark suit and a **TOP HAT** was on display.

"Maybe you can find something special in there," Paulina suggested.

Colette nodded. "Let's take a look!"

As soon as the mouselets stepped inside, though, it was clear this wasn't a typical souvenir shop.

The tiny room was crowded with dark cloaks and **TOP HATS**. The shelves were

Let's go in!

lined with strange books, rings, and batons.

"Why, this is . . ." Violet began.

"The most **famouse** magic shop in Venice!" cried a sharp squeak behind them. A tall, thin mouse EMERGED from the back. "I am Beppe, the owner of the Magic Shop. Welcome!"

"Hey, look!" Colette said, pointing to a small table covered with various MAGICIAN'S objects.

"Those are the thief's cards!" Elisa exclaimed.

Violet turned to Beppe. "Can you tell us about these unusual cards?"

"Certainly. I make them specially for a very **particular** customer . . ."

"What does this customer look like?" Marco asked.

Beppe smiled. "Oh, he's very small, with

lively eyes and lovely black feathers!"

"Are you saying that your customer is . . ." Elisa **sputtered**.

"Yes, he's a **raven**!" the shop owner replied.

A SHOW-STOPPING MESSAGE

The friends scurried outside to discuss their latest discovery. It had been so dark in the magic shop that they were dazzled by the bright sunlight glinting off the canals.

"Holy cheese, our thief is sneakier than a snake in the grass," Pam cried as they began walking along the edge of the canal.

"Yeah," Violet replied. "The magician must have trained the raven so he lets the cards fall, distracting the victim while they hide in the SHADOWS."

Once they had reached Piazza San Marco, Elisa SQUEAKED UP.

"This case keeps getting more intriguing. I'm sorry we CAN'T KEEP working on it . . ."

"Oh, so you are enjoying the mystery, too?" Marco said, SMILING smugly.

"Marco, don't tease me . . ." Elisa began. But just then, the heavy tolling of the bells in the clock tower **interrupted** their conversation.

"Is it noon already?" asked Pam. "It can't be. My stomach hasn't **rumbleD** once!"

"No, it's just a quarter after eleven," Marco replied, checking his **watch**. "I have a feeling something *strange* is going on . . ."

Marco was right. As he squeaked, a small

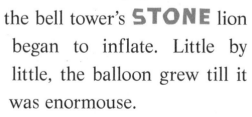

yellow BALLOON next to the bell tower's **STONE** lion began to inflate. Little by little, the balloon grew till it was enormouse.

Everyone in the piazza stopped to *gaze* up at the balloon. The crowd whispered and murmured with surprise.

"What's going on?" asked Elisa.

"I'm afraid we'll find out soon enough," Violet replied. "Look up there!"

A large black raven was *speeding* toward the balloon. The bird gave it a sharp peck with its beak, and a sea of colorful confetti burst from inside.

At that moment, a large banner unfurled from the top of the tower. On it was written:

MY MAGIC WILL STRIKE AGAIN.
WHEN THE EAGLE FLIES, THE MOST
BEAUTIFUL MASK WILL BE MINE!

"It's him! The mysterious thief strikes again!" cried Elisa.

"What a dramatic way to announce his next **theft**," added Paulina. "Quick, let's look around. He must be around here somewhere," she said, turning to scan the crowded square. "But . . . where?"

Violet shook her snout. "We'll never find him in this crowd. If we want to catch the thief, we're going to have to perform a magic trick of our own."

PROFILE OF A THIEF

That afternoon, the mice huddled around a table in an *elegant* café.

"The thief's message said that he would strike '**WHEN THE EAGLE FLIES**,' but what does that mean?" Colette asked.

"My guidebook says the eagle's flight is an event during **Carnival**," Paulina replied.

Elisa and Marco nodded. "Every year, Carnival begins with the Flight of the Angel. It's an ancient tradition. A **mouselet** throws herself off the bell tower in Piazza San Marco," Marco explained. When he saw the Thea Sisters' horrorstruck snouts, he quickly added, "Of course, she always wears a **safety** harness."

Nicky sighed with relief. Then she grinned.

"That's amazing! It must be an unforgettable feeling for the rodent who jumps."

"But the Flight of the Eagle . . . what's that?" asked Pam.

"It's a newer tradition that takes place a week after the Flight of the Angel," explained Marco. "Hundreds of rodents ATTEND. The thief is probably planning to take advantage of the moment when everyone looks up at the eagle. It's the perfect distraction before a *big heist*!"

Just then, the waiter brought them a plate full of golden fritters covered in a dusting of sugar.

"Squeaking of traditions, here are the frittole," Elisa explained.

The group kept chatting as they enjoyed their SNACK. Only two rodents remained quiet: Pam, who was *BUSY* stuffing fritters

into her mouth, and Violet, who was lost in her own thoughts.

Colette noticed. "Everything okay, Vivi?"

She shook her snout. "Oh, yes. I was just thinking about the message from the thief . . ."

"What about it?" asked Elisa.

"I think we should be on the lookout for rodents dressed in magician **costumes**," Violet said.

Paulina began to search her MousePad for photos of magician **costumes**.

Colette peeked at the screen. "They should have an elegant black tuxedo . . . a large cloak . . . and a **TOP HAT**!"

"A magic wand, too, don't you think?" Elisa added.

Nicky sketched a magician costume on a paper napkin.

"You're forgetting something," said Pam. She took Nicky's pen and drew a black bird in flight.

"Right, the raven!" said Marco.

"There's one more clue we should add to this drawing," Elisa said. "Marco, do you remember that show we saw about birds of prey?"

"Of course. It was rattastic!" her brother replied.

Elisa nodded. "The handlers each wore a large glove, to keep the birds' TALONS from hurting them . . ."

"Good clue, Sis!" said Marco. "I'll bet our mysterious thief has a glove like that, or

maybe padding on their shoulder where the raven can perch."

"There we go!" said Pam, adding the glove to the drawing.

"NOW WE KNOW WHAT WE'RE LOOKING FOR!"

HiGH ALERT

Over the next two days, the Thea Sisters and their friends spent their time sightseeing and attending **Carnival**, but their thoughts kept returning to the mysterious thefts of the antique **MASKS** and costumes.

No matter where they went or what they did, the mouselets and Elisa and Marco didn't spot a single rodent dressed as a **MAGICIAN**.

And so, on the third day, it was finally time for the **Flight of the Eagle**. The whole city was on high alert. Marco and Elisa's father had left the house at **dawn** to make sure the police surveillance team was in place.

Elisa and Marco met the **THEA SiSTERS** in the kitchen for a big breakfast. As they ate, the kitchen was so quiet, you could hear a cheese slice drop. All the young mice were thinking about the **mysterious** thief's grand plan.

At last Elisa sighed. "Jumping gerbil babies, this whole mystery is really ruining your vacation."

Marco *laughed*. "So true, Sis. Just look at those long snouts! Good thing we **PLANNED** a surprise for today . . ."

"What surprise?" Violet asked, pricking up her ears.

There's a surprise!

"Oh, nothing," continued Marco, "just tickets to **ATTEND** the Gran Teatro for the Flight of the Eagle.

Plus the final round of the contest for the **most beautiful mask** . . ."

Elisa nodded. "That's right! We have seats in the *parterre*, the area right in front of the stage, so we'll see the masks close up. But . . ." she added, looking at the clock, "we have to hurry: The first round begins at eleven, then the Flight of the Eagle is right after that, and then the next round begins at three o'clock . . ."

"Well, what are we waiting for?" cried Pam. "Let's make like a cheese wheel and roll!"

Once they'd reached Piazza San Marco, the group found seats in front of the stage just in time for the costume parade to begin. They **oohed** and **aahed** as rodents from all over the world strutted past in COSTUMES ranging from traditional to fairy tale and even to totally ridicumouse!

A mouselet in a duck mask was followed

by a mouselet in a dragon costume accompanied by two little mouselings dressed as fiery FLAMES.

Then there were *ladies* and **knights**, kings and queens, and many other spectacular MASKS.

The first group finished, and the stage filled with jugglers and dancers. At last, the long-awaited moment had arrived: It was time for the Flight of the Eagle.

An unearthly silence fell over the square as the shape of a ratlet covered in turquoise feathers appeared on top of the bell tower. A cry of **amazement** rang out from the crowd.

The eagle began to **slide** along the cable

suspended over the piazza. Soon she was soaring over the crowd.

Just then, Pam **noticed** a slight motion out of the corner of her eye. She turned toward one side of the square. "Hey, mouselets!" she cried. "Look down there!"

In a corner, behind a column, stood a figure dressed as a magician. Instead of looking at the eagle like everyone else, he was staring at the side of the stage, where the masked contestants had gathered.

"It's him!" cried Colette. "I'm sure of it!"

The Thea Sisters, Elisa, and Marco *scrambled out* from their seats and raced toward the

mysterious MAGICIAN!

An Unexpected Dive

The magician was just a few steps ahead of the mice, but when they'd almost caught up with him, he started to **RUN**!

The Thea Sisters and their friends *scurried* after him.

"Ugh . . . why . . . does he have to . . . **PUFF** be . . . **PANT** so fast?" asked Pam between strides.

"He must have realized we're following him!" Colette wheezed.

"Come on!" said Paulina. "We gotta stick to him like a glue trap!"

Unfortunately, the magician was *quicker* than a hyperactive hamster on a treadmill. He expertly weaved his way through the throngs, while the mouselets and their friends had to fight their way through.

Nicky, who was the sportiest rat in the group, managed to REACH the magician not far from a wide piazza.

She stretched out a paw to stop him, but the rodent escaped, leaving only a scrap of fabric from his **cloak** in her pawtips!

Got him!

"Over there!" cried Elisa, spotting him again.

The mice STARTED after him. The magician was moving quickly and confidently along the street that bordered the LAGOON.

As they ran, Marco shouted, "If we keep going, we'll end up on the mainland!"

Just then, the magician veered to the **LEFT** and reached a dock where several gondolas were **TIED** up.

"He's going to escape on that boat!" shouted Marco.

Nicky was determined not to let that happen. She *surged* forward to grab him, but the magician stumbled and fell into the **LAGOON**!

"Oh no!" shouted Nicky.

Fortunately, their quarry emerged right away. He was drenched to the fur and a little **disoriented**.

Nicky quickly pulled him out of the icy water. Colette and Elisa ran to get something to **WARM HIM** up.

"At last we've **caught** you," Pam cried.

The magician's eyes widened. "What are you talking about?"

"Don't pretend with us," said Marco sternly. "You play with the rat, you get the tail! We know who you are!"

"Who I am?! But I've never seen you before! What do you want from me?"

"We want you to confess!" Paulina urged him.

"Confess? To what . . . ACHOO!"

Just then, Elisa and Colette returned from a nearby hotel, where they'd gone to ask for **HELP**.

They were carrying a thick blanket, which they wrapped around the magician, and a thermos of hot tea.

"Thank you . . ." he said in a thin squeak.

Once he'd recovered, the magician removed

his mask. He was a ratlet around the same age as the mouselets, and he was dazed by his sudden dip in the canal.

Suddenly, Colette realized this wasn't the FIRST time they'd seen him. "Wait a minute, I know you! You're the ratlet who played tour guide for us when we took our first boat ride in Venice!"

The other mouselets looked at him in disbelief. "It's true! Can it be . . .

that you're the THIEF?"

A REAL BLUNDER

The ratlet **LOOKED** up at the mouselets' curious snouts. "That's right, now I remember you . . . you're the ones who couldn't take your **EYES** off your MousePad."

Marco was getting impatient. "Okay, so you've already MET. That's nice. But now we need to know why you've been going around stealing masks."

"I haven't stolen anything!" the ratlet protested.

"If you ask me, you're the ones who owe *me* an explanation. Why were you following me? You made me fall into the canal, which wasn't exactly a pleasant experience, especially at this time of year!"

"Sorry . . ." Nicky replied. "I was a bit hasty . . . maybe we all jumped to the *wrong* conclusion . . ."

"No way. His story smells fishier than day-old tuna," Pam interrupted. "He must be the thief, otherwise why was he running away?"

"Running away? Who says I was running away?" he replied.

"Well, once you noticed us, you started to *RUN* . . ."

The ratlet's whiskers began quivering with laughter.

"What's so funny?" Marco asked, a bit annoyed.

"It wasn't a chase. It was a race!" the ratlet said.

"What do you mean?!" Elisa asked.

"During Carnival, I always have a race with my two best friends. One is the MOTORBOAT driver. Do you remember him?"

The Thea Sisters nodded.

"We've known each other since we were little, and we always play JOKES on each other. Every year, as soon as the Flight of the Eagle ends, we take off from different spots in the piazza. We each make our way to a dock and take a gondola through the canals until we reach Verezia Santa Lucia station. Whoever arrives first wins!"

"What a weird tradition," Violet said.

"We think it's fun," the ratlet said, getting up. He took off his soaked cloak and shook off the last drops of water from his costume.

"Then you weren't the one who stole **Berto Del Bon's** masks . . ." said Elisa.

"Berto Del Bon? Who's that?"

"And you don't have a tame **Raven** . . ." added Colette.

"I didn't even know that ravens *could* be **TAMED**!"

"I'm sorry, I guess we made a mistake," Marco said, shaking his snout in **disappointment**. "We got the wrong end of the cheese stick this time."

"Yeah . . ." the ratlet said. "And now, if you'll excuse me, I'd like to head for the station. I know I've already lost the race, but whoever arrives last has to do favors for the others until next year's Carnival!"

"So because of us . . ." Nicky began.

"I lost the race," the ratlet said.

"AND IT SOUNDS LIKE YOU'VE LOST YOUR THIEF!"

ONE MAGICIAN, TWO MAGICIANS . . . TOO MANY MAGICIANS!

The friends headed back toward Piazza San Marco, *dragging* their tails behind them.

"Papa was right. We should never have gotten involved!" Elisa said. "All we've done is made a muddle of things."

"But the suspect fit the profile! He was dressed like a magician, and it sure looked like he was **fleeing** the scene," Marco pointed out.

"Well," Violet said, "following this lead took us far away from the scene of the crime. **Look!**"

Sure enough, the Gran Teatro was in a state of panic and **confusion**.

All the contestants from the costume parade were crowded onstage, milling around in distress. The police inspector stood among them, surrounded by other officers.

"There's Papa . . . the **THEFT** must have already taken place!" Marco observed.

Paulina noticed that the mouselet dressed like a dragon was in tears. She was no longer wearing her splendid **mask**!

A few of the other contestants were trying to comfort her.

They'll find it!

"So the thief stole the dragon mask," Paulina said.

The Thea Sisters and their friends tried to get the INSPECTOR'S attention, but he was busy talking to one of his officers. Soon, though, the inspector scrambled down and headed toward them.

"SEE?" said Marco. "Now we'll be able to give Papa and his colleagues a paw."

But he was wrong. "Marco, Elisa, please go home," the inspector said firmly. "I don't want you and your friends mixed up in this mess."

Disappointed, the Thea Sisters and Marco and Elisa turned to leave. But suddenly, a bright light blinded the crowd. Then a garbled squeak came from the Gran Teatro's loudsqueaker:

"NOW MY MISSION IS COMPLETE, AND YOU'LL NEVER FIND ME!"

When their **EYES** cleared, they realized a shower of **CONFETTI** was falling from the sky. A dark figure in a long cloak appeared in one corner of the piazza.

"*Quick, that way!*" shouted the inspector, running off stage.

A moment later, the magician materialized on the opposite side of the square, and the inspector turned on his heel to **CHASE** him. But he spun around so quickly that he fell and hurt his ankle!

"Papa!" shouted Elisa, running over to him.

"It's just sprained, don't **worry**," the inspector said, getting up. But the **PAIN** stopped him. "Go on, you go!" he shouted to his officers.

But the magician had **disappeared** again.

ow!

"Look, down there!" an officer shouted, pointing to a dark **shape** *flickering* at the end of an alley. The **OFFICERS** began running toward it. Marco was about to start pursuing it, too, but Violet stopped him.

"Our magician likes sleights of paw, false leads, misdirection . . . I'm sure this is another trick to **mislead** everyone."

"I think you're right, Vivi," Nicky added. "Look up there!"

A black spot was fluttering around the bell tower. Squinting, the friends could make out the shape of a bird flying up to the top of the tower.

THE RAVEN'S FLIGHT

"The raven is **flying** up the bell tower!" cried Marco.

"Come on, move those tails!" Nicky urged her friends. She hurried toward the tower. "We can't let him escape!"

When they crossed the tower's threshold, the mice were in for a **shock**: The elevator that usually took tourists to the top had stopped on the ground floor. It was **OUT OF SERVICE**!

"He must have sabotaged it," said Colette. "To keep us from following him . . ."

Violet shook her snout. "But the elevator is right here, so the **magician** couldn't have used it . . ."

Elisa knew what to do. She threw open a small door. "This is where he went! The stairs!"

The Thea Sisters and their friends raced toward the steps and began to CLIMB.

Halfway up, though, only Nicky and Marco were able to keep pace. The others lagged behind, breathing hard.

"Come on, mouselets!" Nicky called after she spotted something dark twirling on the steps ahead of her. "We're almost there! The magician is almost at the top, I can see his cloak!"

Pam tried to speed up, but she stopped after a few steps. "You go ahead . . . PUFF, PUFF . . . go on!"

Nicky and Marco exchanged a quick look. Then they both *rushed* toward the magician. With one last burst of energy, they reached the top of the tower.

The magician had climbed up onto a pedestal and ripped through the safety net that covered the windows facing the piazza. His faithful **raven** was outside circling the top of the tower.

"Stop!" Nicky shouted. "We've caught you, and we're not going to let you escape!"

The rodent turned toward the mice, his cloak waving in the wind. "Ha, ha, ha!

That's what you think!"

With a dramatic flourish, he uncovered a contraption on the ground next to him.

"Oh no! He has a hang glider! He's going to use it to escape!" Nicky cried.

Marco leaped into action faster than a mousetrap spring. He reached into his pocket and pulled out a pawful of confetti, which he threw right into the magician's **EYES**.

You won't escape!

"You think you're the only one who knows how to do **tricks**?" he shouted.

"Now!" Marco hissed to Nicky. "Let's sabotage the hang glider!"

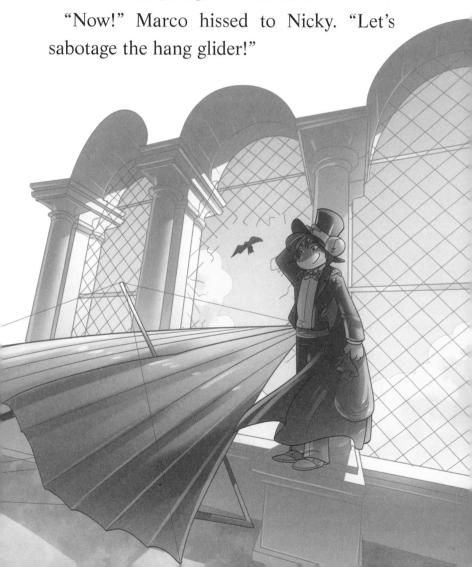

Nicky didn't have to be told twice: With one long step, she'd **reached** the hang glider and then started snapping the rods supporting the wings.

"Noooooooo!" the magician shouted as he watched his plans crumble like feta cheese.

Just then, Elisa and the other Thea Sisters reached the top of the bell tower. When they realized what was happening, they helped their friends **WRECK** the hang glider and stop the thief.

"Now your magic tricks won't help you," cried Marco with a satisfied smile.

The magician let out a LONG SIGH.

"We did it!" Pam cried. "We caught the thief!"

THIEF . . . OR COLLECTOR?

Colette noticed that there was a dark bag on the ground **next** to the hang glider. She scurried over and peeked inside. "Hey, **LOOK**!" she said, pulling the stolen dragon mask out of the bag.

"Stop! Don't touch that," the magician shouted.

As he squeaked, the raven **swooped** toward Colette, forcing her to back off.

She cried out in fear and let go of the mask, which **tumbled** toward the ground.

A moment before it hit, Nicky caught the

precious mask. "Saved!" she cried.

"Paws off! That **mask** is mine, it belongs to me!" the magician sputtered.

"Has the cheese slipped off your cracker? That mask isn't yours. It belongs to the mouselet you STOLE it from," Pam corrected him.

The magician shook his snout. "You don't understand what's really going on." The raven

Got it!

swooped down again, this time coming to perch on his shoulder. "I'm no common thief. All my crimes have special targets . . ." he began to explain.

"We know," Violet said. "You steal only masks and costumes designed by **Berto Del Bon**."

The magician was surprised. "So you *do* know . . ."

"Yes, but that doesn't change the fact that you're guilty!" Elisa said.

"Is it a crime to follow the wishes of your own your ancestor?" the magician replied enigmatically.

"Ancestor?!" Nicky said. "Wait a minute . . ."

The magician nodded. "Yes, that's right. I'm a descendant of the great Berto Del Bon, an artist who wasn't lucky enough to be appreciated in his own time. The Venetians treated him with arrogance and disdain. They weren't WORTHY of his creations!"

"Are you saying that you've been stealing your ancestor's creations . . . for revenge?" Violet asked.

Take it away!

The magician nodded. "That's right! After Berto Del Bon offended the **richest** and most arrogant merchant in the city with a **turkey** mask, everyone turned their tails on him. This city never **HONORED** him like it should have!"

"And you think you can preserve his creations by hiding them away?!" Paulina asked in disbelief.

You're too late!

"I'm not hiding them. I'm creating a collection of the highest level. Now I'm just missing a single **mask** . . ." the thief trailed off.

"I'll bet you're talking about the one at the

Murano Glass Museum," Violet said.

"You've guessed it . . . but you're too late!" the thief cried.

With that, he tossed his **TOP HAT** in the air . . . and a thick blue fog streamed out of it!

"Cough, cough . . ." the mice wheezed, waving their paws around to clear away the cloud of gas. The squawking of the raven sounded farther and farther away as the magician disappeared once more!

THE MAGIC IS OVER!

"I can't believe this," moaned Pam. "He's escaped again!"

The friends RUSHED down the stairs, one flight after another, until they reached the bottom of the bell tower. There they were forced to stop. At the exit, a familiar figure had blocked the thief's escape!

"Papa!" Marco and Elisa cried. "You're here . . ."

For the first time that day, the inspector turned to his children with a big smile on his snout.

"But . . . but how did you know?" Marco asked in awe.

"I followed your HUNCH," the inspector said.

"What do you mean?" asked Elisa.

"I was sitting in a corner of the piazza, resting my ankle, when I spotted a **raven** flying around the bell tower. I immediately remembered what you told me about the feather and the flapping wings, and the **COINCIDENCE** was just too huge!"

"So you trusted our instincts," Elisa said.

This isn't over!

The **inspector** nodded. "I knew the thief couldn't be far away. So I *hurried* over here, and I arrived just in the nick of time, as you can see!" he **concluded**, pawcuffing the **magician**.

"This time, the magic is really over," declared Colette.

The magician hung his snout, which was missing his **TOP HAT**.

The raven fluttered above them. "We should call the Animal Protection Society," said Nicky. "We can't just abandon a tame **raven**."

"Of course. We'll send someone to **take care of it** shortly," the inspector declared as a group of his officers joined them.

"Thank you, **MOUSELETS**, for your help," the inspector said. "I was too hard on you. You have all been great **DETECTIVES**."

That made Marco blush with pride. Pam grinned at him.

The magician gave the young mice one last **bitter** smile. Then the officers wheeled him around and escorted him to the police station.

"What an incorrigible rodent," said Colette,

shaking her blond fur.

"LOOK!" cried Elisa, pointing to a spot above their heads. The raven, now alone, **was flying** around in circles, looking lost.

Nicky SLOWLY drew closer and called to it. She'd had training in dealing with wild animals from the Green Mice, an environmental organization she and Paulina belonged to. Soon, the bird flew **closer**.

"Is it me, or is there something in its talons?" Pam asked.

"It looks like a **card**," cried Marco.

The raven opened its **talons** and let the card fall.

Pam grabbed it. "Good Gouda! This isn't the **USUAL** top hat card."

The friends gathered around to look at the new clue.

"It's the **image** of a bridge with a female rodent . . ." said Nicky.

"It's a mouselet who's laughing . . . or maybe yawning . . . or . . ." Pam continued.

"I think she's **sighing**," said Colette.

Elisa smiled. "It's the Bridge of Sighs!"

THE BRIDGE OF SIGHS

This was an UNEXPECTED clue. The Thea Sisters and their friends stared at it in silence for a moment.

"But what does it mean?" asked Paulina.

"I don't understand . . ." Elisa replied. "I thought we'd solved the mystery!"

"Maybe the Bridge of Sighs has some connection to the thefts," Marco suggested.

What does it mean?

"Yes, you're right. It must be a **lead**," said Colette. "Should we go check it out?"

Elisa shook her snout. "Unfortunately, we can't. We have to settle for looking at it from a DISTANCE.

You see, you can't cross the Bridge of Sighs unless you're visiting the buildings connected to it."

"But we can get as close as possible," said Marco. "There are two larger bridges nearby. We can go there."

The group *hurried away*.

The Bridge of Sighs wasn't far from Piazza San Marco. A few minutes later, the rodents had reached their destination.

"There it is," cried Elisa, pointing to a small, elegant covered bridge not far from where they stood.

"It's beautiful, but I don't understand what it has to do with our thief," said Colette.

"Let's take a look from the other side . . . come on!" Marco suggested.

The young mice scurried to another nearby bridge, but they didn't notice anything

unusual from there, either.

"Maybe it's just another one of the magician's tricks," Violet said.

"Yes, there's probably nothing to uncover here. We should just go BACK home," said Elisa.

But just then, Nicky cried, "Wait, I think I found something!"

On the window of one of the buildings nearby was a drawing of a small black raven wearing a TOP HAT.

"Nice work, Nick!" cried Pam. "Come on, let's go see what's hiding there."

After a quick scan of the area, Paulina noticed there was a small warehouse on the other side of the window. But the ENTRANCE was tightly sealed.

"How strange . . . there isn't even a keyhole," Violet observed. "There's just this strange crack."

"I have an idea," said Nicky.

She grasped the CARD that had led them there and inserted it into the crack. With a **click**, the door opened.

"Now we're cooking with cheese!" Pam cheered.

"I CAN'T WAIT TO FIND OUT WHAT'S INSIDE!"

THE FINAL TRICK

Colette, Nicky, Pam, Paulina, Violet, Elisa, and Marco found themselves in a **LARGE** room that was nearly empty, except for a few shelves filled with **TOP HATS** and books about ravens.

"This must be the magician's **lair**," breathed Paulina.

Marco spotted a small machine that looked like a **CAMERA**. Cautiously, he pushed a button on the top. A **RAY** of light came out of the machine, projecting the image of a jeweled pin onto the floor.

"That's how he created objects that suddenly disappeared," Paulina said.

"Hey, check this out," said Elisa. In the middle of the room was a large **TRUNK** with the key sticking out of the lock.

"Maybe it's the chest where he keeps his treasures," suggested Colette. "Come on, let's try to open it."

The friends gathered around it, **excited**, and Marco turned the key.

Instantly, the room went **dark**. The air filled with the **NOISY** squawks of a flock of ravens. The rodents covered their snouts with their paws to protect themselves.

"Aaah!" Colette squeaked.

"Help!" squealed Elisa, stooping behind her brother, who was waving his paws around to try to scare off the swarm of birds swooping around them.

But then the mice all *realized* something simultaneously: The ravens weren't REAL!

"Wait," cried Nicky, calming down. "It's just another **trick**!"

Pam switched on the light, and everyone took a good look around. All the windows in the room were covered by heavy **black curtains**, making the room really dark. The ravens were an illusion — a trick created by **ropes** with large pieces of black cloth attached.

"Wow, that was pretty **CREEPY** . . ." Colette said, smoothing her messed-up fur.

"Yeah," Nicky said, "but I don't understand. What *triggered* the fake ravens?"

"I'm pretty sure they were activated when Marco **turned** the key in the lock," Paulina said. "Let's try turning it `counterclockwise` instead of clockwise."

Marco **nodded** and did as Paulina suggested. This time, the trunk opened right

away. There were *no more surprises* . . .
except for one: It was completely empty!

LET'S FIGURE IT OUT!

The Thea Sisters, Elisa, and Marco couldn't hold back sighs of disappointment. It looked like the magician had played another trick on them.

"I can't believe it!" Elisa lamented. "After all that work, we found a whole lot of nothing."

"Keep calm and scurry on, rodents! I'll bet there's another clue here. Let's try to figure it out," Colette said.

Paulina was doubtful. "There's not much to figure out, Coco. This trunk is just another one of the magician's tricks."

"You're right," Marco replied. "The thief has played another joke on us!"

"Actually, I think Coco is right," said Violet. "Until now, the thief's 'magic' has just been a series of well-constructed tricks, right?"

The others agreed.

"Then the empty chest must be one, too," said Nicky.

"That can't be," replied Marco. "Take a look. There's NOTHING inside!"

"Should we try to lift it?" asked Pam.

THE MAGICIAN'S TRICKS

1. Projections that SIMULATE valuable objects
2. A raven to DISTRACT the targets
3. A top hat that ACTIVATES a cloud of smoke
4. FAKE ravens activated by the key to the chest

"Maybe there's something underneath."

The rodents tried lifting the chest, but it was too **heavy** and **HUGE**.

"I want to take a closer **LOOK** from inside," Elisa said at last. "I'll just climb in. There's plenty of room for a rodent inside that thing."

"Don't even think about it," her brother said. "You could get hurt. We don't know what other tricks our **THIEF** may have cooked up."

"Don't worry, I'll be careful," said Elisa.

"Besides, I *won't be alone.*" She placed a paw inside the chest and took a tentative step inside. A moment later, she let out a shout.

Marco instinctively leaped toward her, but Pam stopped him. The shout had transformed into a . . . big laugh!

"You'll never believe it! There's A MIRROR in here," Elisa replied.

"A mirror?!" said Nicky in disbelief.

"That's right! I saw a figure in the shadows and I was TERRIFIED . . . but it was just my reflection!"

"I don't understand," said Pam. "Why is there A MIRROR inside?"

Elisa shook her snout. "The mirror is tilted and DIVIDES the chest in two, on a diagonal. That means that it reflects the two dark sides, so the chest looks empty. But only one half is empty! Look!"

Elisa showed Marco and the Thea Sisters the mirror, and the mice realized that there was an 𝖎𝖓𝖛𝖎𝖘𝖎𝖇𝖑𝖊 opening. They opened it and discovered . . . the thief's hiding place!

"Chewy chocolate cheesecake!" cried Pam. "All the stolen MASKS and costumes are inside."

One by one, the friends pulled out the

Look at this!

objects the thief had plundered during Carnival.

Violet smiled.

"THIS TIME THE TRICK'S ON HIM!"

THE BEST SOLUTION

The mouselets and their friends called the inspector, and he had his officers bring the stolen costumes and masks to the police station. All the rodents who'd had something stolen came to collect their possessions. The inspector even managed to track down the rodent who'd lost her fan.

The friends explained who the thief was and why he had set his sights on their masks and accessories.

". . . so now your items can be returned to you," the inspector declared.

"Finally!" cried the rodent who'd had her winter headpiece stolen.

Everyone seemed satisfied to have their possessions back . . . everyone except the elderly rodent from **MURANO**.

"Is something wrong?" Colette asked kindly once she saw his **worried** look.

"Well . . . I was thinking that the thief wasn't entirely wrong."

"**Whaaaaat?!**" cried the rodent whose fan had been stolen. "What do you mean?"

"Well, Venice has never honored the great **Berto Del Bon**. He was a very skilled artist with a noble spirit . . ." the elderly rodent explained.

"That's true," the owner of the golden **costume** said. "I've heard the legend of the turkey mask, and I must say I've always taken the side of poor **Del Bon!**"

"That's true, he was a talented artist who never got his ⅮⓊⒺ, but there's nothing we can do about it now," said the rodent with the fan. "Is there?"

The Thea Sisters exchanged a **LOOK**. They were all having the same idea.

Colette cleared her throat. "Here in *Venice* we've admired your city's unique beauty, your delicious local cooking, the festive traditions of *Carnival* . . . and also your many museums!"

"That's right," added Paulina. "And what better way to preserve a collection than in a *museum*? Wouldn't it be great if rodents could come admire the works of this great Venetian master?"

"What are you saying? We should **gather up** our costumes and masks in a museum dedicated to **Berto Del Bon**?" asked the rodent with the fan.

The mouselets nodded. "Yes, exactly!"

"Actually, I own a BUiLDiNG that could be turned into a museum," the INSPECTOR'S friend said.

"It's a wonderful idea . . . and I will donate my services as curator!" the rodent from Murano put in.

After squeaking it over for a few minutes,

It's a great idea!

Let's do it!

Hooray!

the rodents came to an *agreement.* Instead of being stowed away in their closets, the works of Berto Del Bon would be placed in a museum dedicated to his craft.

Of course!

"On one condition, though," added the rodent with the fan.

"What's that?" asked the inspector.

"That each of us can borrow back our own costumes for Carnival, of course."

The inspector smiled. "Agreed!

We'll always respect our Carnival TRADITIONS."

FAREWELL, VENICE!

At last the mystery of the thief had been solved, and there was a new home for the STOLEN GOODS that everyone could agree on.

"It's a good lesson for the magician, too. There are ways to pay respect to the memory of your ancestors without doing something ILLEGAL," Colette said as she and her friends walked to Piazza San Marco.

The Mardi Gras grand parade was just starting. Since it marked the end of Carnival, the Thea Sisters had changed into costumes for the occasion.

"It's so magical here . . ." Pam sighed as they joined the crowd. "Between the beauty of the city, the excitement of the

investigation, and the fun of Carnival, there hasn't been a dull moment!"

"You never get bored in Venice," said Marco, smiling. "I hope you'll all remember that and come back to see us again."

"You can count on it!" said Pam.

And with that, the friends plunged into the happy Carnival crowd for one last time . . . at least for this year!

**Thea Stilton and the
Lost Letters**

**Thea Stilton and the
Tropical Treasure**

**Thea Stilton and the
Hollywood Hoax**

**Thea Stilton and the
Madagascar Madness**

**Thea Stilton and the
Frozen Fiasco**

**Thea Stilton and the
Venice Masquerade**

**Thea Stilton and the
Niagara Splash**

And check out my fabumouse special editions!

**THEA STILTON:
THE JOURNEY
TO ATLANTIS**

**THEA STILTON:
THE SECRET OF
THE FAIRIES**

**THEA STILTON:
THE SECRET OF
THE SNOW**

**THEA STILTON:
THE CLOUD
CASTLE**

**THEA STILTON:
THE TREASURE
OF THE SEA**

**THEA STILTON:
THE LAND OF
FLOWERS**

Be sure to read all my fabumouse adventures!

#1 Lost Treasure of the Emerald Eye

#2 The Curse of the Cheese Pyramid

#3 Cat and Mouse in a Haunted House

#4 I'm Too Fond of My Fur!

#5 Four Mice Deep in the Jungle

#6 Paws Off, Cheddarface!

#7 Red Pizzas for a Blue Count

#8 Attack of the Bandit Cats

#9 A Fabumouse Vacation for Geronimo

#10 All Because of a Cup of Coffee

#11 It's Halloween, You 'Fraidy Mouse!

#12 Merry Christmas, Geronimo!

#13 The Phantom of the Subway

#14 The Temple of the Ruby of Fire

#15 The Mona Mousa Code

#16 A Cheese-Colored Camper

#17 Watch Your Whiskers, Stilton!

#18 Shipwreck on the Pirate Islands

#19 My Name Is Stilton, Geronimo Stilton

#20 Surf's Up, Geronimo!

#21 The Wild, Wild West

#22 The Secret of Cacklefur Castle

A Christmas Tale

#23 Valentine's Day Disaster | **#24 Field Trip to Niagara Falls** | **#25 The Search for Sunken Treasure** | **#26 The Mummy with No Name** | **#27 The Christmas Toy Factory**

#28 Wedding Crasher | **#29 Down and Out Down Under** | **#30 The Mouse Island Marathon** | **#31 The Mysterious Cheese Thief** | **Christmas Catastrophe**

#32 Valley of the Giant Skeletons | **#33 Geronimo and the Gold Medal Mystery** | **#34 Geronimo Stilton, Secret Agent** | **#35 A Very Merry Christmas** | **#36 Geronimo's Valentine**

#37 The Race Across America | **#38 A Fabumouse School Adventure** | **#39 Singing Sensation** | **#40 The Karate Mouse** | **#41 Mighty Mount Kilimanjaro**

#42 The Peculiar Pumpkin Thief | **#43 I'm Not a Supermouse!** | **#44 The Giant Diamond Robbery** | **#45 Save the White Whale!** | **#46 The Haunted Castle**

#47 Run for the Hills, Geronimo!

#48 The Mystery in Venice

#49 The Way of the Samurai

#50 This Hotel Is Haunted!

#51 The Enormouse Pearl Heist

#52 Mouse in Space!

#53 Rumble in the Jungle

#54 Get into Gear, Stilton!

#55 The Golden Statue Plot

#56 Flight of the Red Bandit

#57 The Stinky Cheese Vacation

#58 The Super Chef Contest

#59 Welcome to Moldy Manor

#60 The Treasure of Easter Island

#61 Mouse House Hunter

#62 Mouse Overboard!

#63 The Cheese Experiment

#64 Magical Mission

#65 Bollywood Burglary

#66 Operation: Secret Recipe

#67 The Chocolate Chase

#68 Cyber-Thief Showdown

Up Next!

#69 Hug a Tree, Geronimo

Don't miss any of my adventures in the Kingdom of Fantasy!

THE KINGDOM OF FANTASY

THE QUEST FOR PARADISE:
THE RETURN TO THE KINGDOM OF FANTASY

THE AMAZING VOYAGE:
THE THIRD ADVENTURE IN THE KINGDOM OF FANTASY

THE DRAGON PROPHECY:
THE FOURTH ADVENTURE IN THE KINGDOM OF FANTASY

THE VOLCANO OF FIRE:
THE FIFTH ADVENTURE IN THE KINGDOM OF FANTASY

THE SEARCH FOR TREASURE:
THE SIXTH ADVENTURE IN THE KINGDOM OF FANTASY

THE ENCHANTED CHARMS:
THE SEVENTH ADVENTURE IN THE KINGDOM OF FANTASY

THE PHOENIX OF DESTINY:
AN EPIC KINGDOM OF FANTASY ADVENTURE

THE HOUR OF MAGIC:
THE EIGHTH ADVENTURE IN THE KINGDOM OF FANTASY

THE WIZARD'S WAND:
THE NINTH ADVENTURE IN THE KINGDOM OF FANTASY

THE SHIP OF SECRETS:
THE TENTH ADVENTURE IN THE KINGDOM OF FANTASY

THE DRAGON OF FORTUNE:
AN EPIC KINGDOM OF FANTASY ADVENTURE

Meet
CREEPELLA VON CACKLEFUR

I, *Geronimo Stilton*, have a lot of mouse friends, but none as **spooky** as my friend CREEPELLA VON CACKLEFUR! She is an enchanting and MYSTERIOUS mouse with a pet bat named **Bitewing**. YIKES! I'm a real 'fraidy mouse, but even I think CREEPELLA and her family are AWFULLY fascinating. I can't wait for you to read all about CREEPELLA in these fa-mouse-ly funny and **spectacularly spooky** tales!

#1 The Thirteen Ghosts

#2 Meet Me in Horrorwood

#3 Ghost Pirate Treasure

#4 Return of the Vampire

#5 Fright Night

#6 Ride for Your Life!

#7 A Suitcase Full of Ghosts

#8 The Phantom of the Theater

#9 The Haunted Dinosaur

THANKS FOR READING, AND GOOD-BYE UNTIL OUR NEXT ADVENTURE!